Hans Helgesen Elementary School,
4983 Rocky Point Road,
R.R. #2, Victoria, B.C.
V9B 5B4

GRE	Greaves, Margaret
E	Mouse Mischief
	1698 16.95

Hans Helgesen Elementary School,
4983 Rocky Point Road,
R.R. #2, Victoria, B.C.
V9B 5B4

Mouse Mischief

story by
Margaret Greaves

pictures by
Jane Pinkney

MB

MARILYN MALIN BOOKS
IN ASSOCIATION WITH ANDRE DEUTSCH

Libby was so naughty in school that she was kept in.
"Amanda will be flying her kite by now," she said sadly
to herself, "and Pipkin will be fishing for tadpoles."

But soon she was free to join the others.
"Watch me, I'm a juggler!" said Pipkin, tossing up the
ivy berries.

Then a car shot round the corner.
"Look out, Pipkin! Run!" shouted Amanda. Pipkin jumped out of the way, but they were all frightened.

"You know we mustn't play in the road," said Libby. "Let's hope no one tells Mother."

"I won't do it again," promised Pipkin. He was very scared too. And they all scampered home as quick as a flash.

Their sister Lucy was to be married the very next day.
She was admiring herself in the beautiful dress she
would wear after the wedding.

"Let's dress up!" said Libby. But soon they were bored.

"I'm going to play marbles," said Pipkin. He let them go bump from one step to the other.

"And I'll practise my violin in the attic,"said Amanda. But she was only a beginner and made quite terrible noises.

"Whatever is all that noise?" called their mother crossly. "Bumping on the stairs and squealing! I've got enough to do, getting ready for the wedding. Play quietly for goodness, sake." The mouse children knew she was really cross.

"Sorry," said Amanda quickly. "I'll look after the babies for a bit if you like."

The others tried to be quiet and keep out of the way.
Libby teased the china cat with a china mouse.

She put on her hat and coat and she and
Pipkin took turns on the rocking horse.

Then Libby had another idea. "Let's play in the bathroom," she said. "I want to float my boat." But she got in the bath as well, and all the water slopped out.

"Pipkin and I can blow bubbles," said Amanda. "Turn the tap on, Pipkin."

They made beautiful bubbles, but Pipkin forgot to turn off the tap. Soon the bathroom was in a terrible mess.

"Whatever can we do?" wailed Amanda. "Mother will be furious."

"We'll use the big towels to mop it up," said Pipkin. They used all the towels they could find, and the bath mat too. Then they took them out to dry on the washing line. Pipkin swung on the line for fun, but the wind nearly blew him away – and he nearly brought the line down.

"Come in at once, you naughty children!" called their mother. She was very angry. "I can't turn my back for a minute without trouble. If you can't be good you shan't go to the wedding."
That was too dreadful! So Libby helped to clear up, and make the house pretty for the wedding.

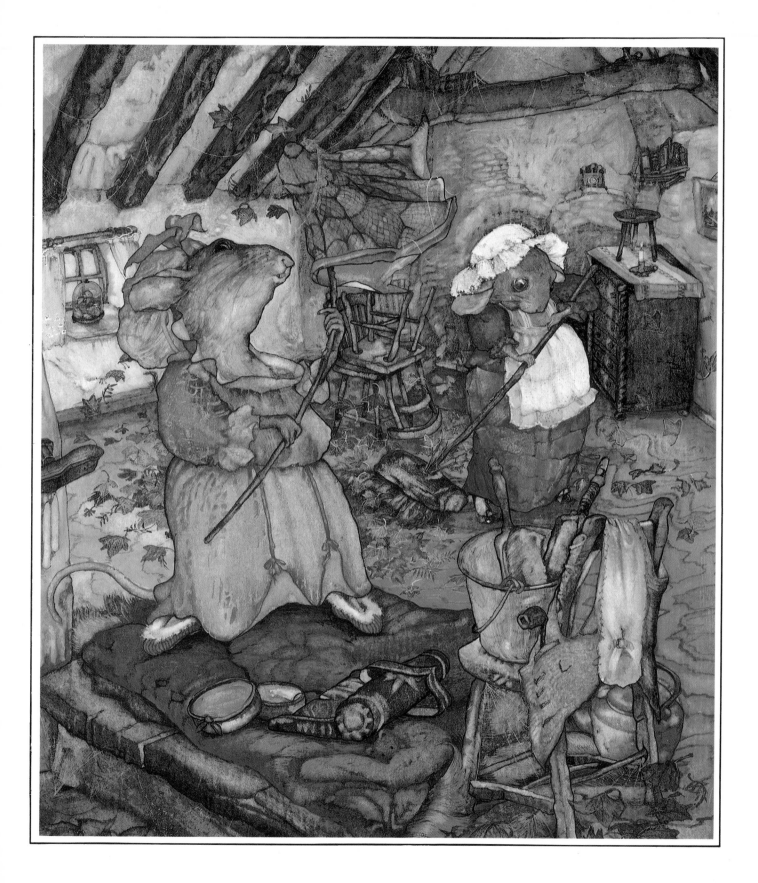

Amanda and Pipkin played quietly for once at being doctor and nurse. Then it was time to prepare the wedding feast.

Next day all the grown-up mice wore their best clothes for the wedding. Lucy was very shy as she and the bridegroom greeted all the guests.

After the wedding there was a wonderful party in the garden, with crackers and paper hats for all the children.

Pipkin pulled his cracker much too hard and sat down very suddenly in a bowl of strawberries. Amanda and Libby were chasing each other round and round the tables.

After the party, Amanda had a good idea.

"We'll tidy everything up and give Mother a nice surprise," she said.

It *was* a good idea, until Pipkin started juggling with the plates and Libby dropped a jug and broke it.

"It's all gone wrong," said Amanda, and they all wanted to cry.

"Never mind," said their mother, "at least you tried to be helpful. Now it's time for little mice to be in bed."

She tucked them all up, and said goodnight. And the moon shone down on
    Amanda
        and Libby
            and Pipkin . . .
                all fast asleep and dreaming.

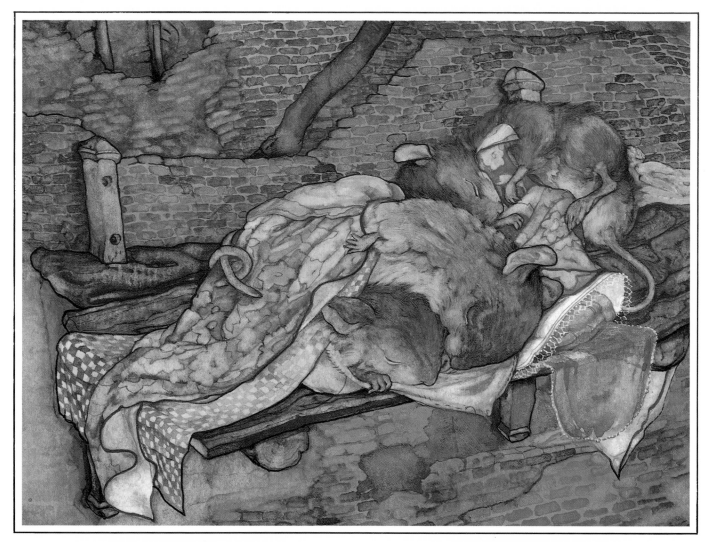

First published in 1989 by MARILYN MALIN BOOKS
in association with ANDRE DEUTSCH LTD
105–106 Great Russell Street, London WC1B 3LJ

Illustrations copyright © 1989 by Jane Pinkney
Text copyright © 1989 by Margaret Greaves

British Library Cataloguing in Publication Data

Greaves, Margaret
Mouse mischief.
I. Title II. Pinkney, Jane
823'.914 [J]

ISBN 0 233 98118 7